TOM
AND THE ISLAND OF
DINOSAURS

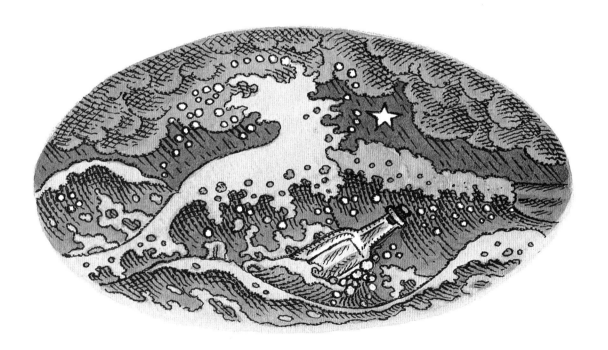

IAN BECK

PICTURE CORGI BOOKS

This one is for

Philippa Dickinson

A PICURE CORGI BOOK: 978 0 552 56624 7

First published in Great Britain by Doubleday 1993
Picture Corgi edition published 1995

14 16 18 20 19 17 15 13 12

Text copyright © Ian Beck 1993

The right of Ian Beck to be identified as the author of this
work has been asserted in accordance with the Copyright, Designs and Patents Act 1988

Picture Corgi Books are published by Random House Children's Books,
61-63 Uxbridge Road, London W5 5SA,
a division of The Random House Group Ltd.

Addresses for companies within The Random House Group Limited
can be found at: www.randomhouse.co.uk/offices.htm

THE RANDOM HOUSE GROUP Limited Reg No. 954009
www.**kidsatrandomhouse**.co.uk

A CIP catalogue record for this book is available from the British Library.

Printed in China

There once was a boy called Tom, who lived
with his grandfather in an old lighthouse
at the edge of the sea.

Between them, Tom and his grandfather
took care of the lighthouse.

On stormy days and moonless nights,
they would light the lamp to show
passing ships where the rocks were.

On sunny days, they would go fishing together
and Tom's grandfather would tell him wonderful
stories of faraway lands and sea monsters.

Tom loved his grandfather and the lighthouse
very much, but sometimes he longed to sail
the wide, grey seas in search of adventure.

One day, Tom saw something glinting among
the wet pebbles on the seashore. It was an old
bottle, chipped and covered with seaweed,
with a message inside.

Tom rushed home with the message.
"Oh, poor girl!" said his grandfather.
"She's in terrible trouble." He looked worried.
"But what can we do? We can't leave the
lighthouse. If a storm blows up
we'll have to light the lamp."
"Don't worry, Grandfather," said Tom.
"I'll rescue her."

Tom raced down the stairs to fetch the special emergency box.

He pushed and pulled and heaved it up the narrow steps to the

balcony. He pulled the ripcord. With a rush of wind, the sides of

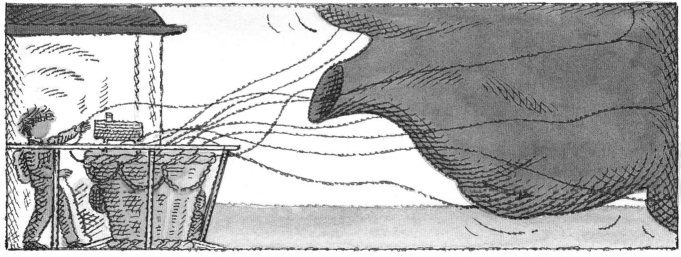

the box collapsed and an enormous rescue balloon filled with air.

Tom jumped into the basket. His grandfather
gave him a snack for the journey and
wished him luck.
"Be careful," he said, as he let the tether go.

Tom's balloon soared into the sky. As night fell,
he drifted across cold seas and sleeping towns.

He flew past snow-covered mountains,

across wild, dark green forests,

through rainstorms and over waterfalls.

At times, the balloon dipped down to touch the waves.

Later, it drifted across a great city at dawn,

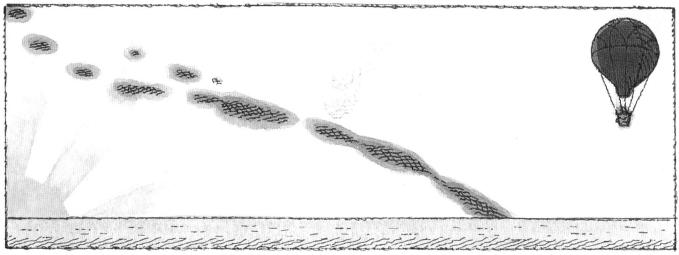

and then, as the sun rose, flew on far, far away.

At last Tom could see the island below him.
A ship lay wrecked on the rocks, but there
was no sign of Katy or the dinosaurs.
Great belches of smoke and fire rose
from the volcano.

He let the balloon drift down through the
swirling smoke and fixed the anchor to a tree.
He climbed down and began to look for Katy.

Just then, he heard someone calling him.
It was Katy! She was perched high up in a tree.
"Quick!" Tom shouted. "We've got to get
out of here. The volcano is about to erupt!"

"We can't go yet," said Katy.
"Come and look at this..."

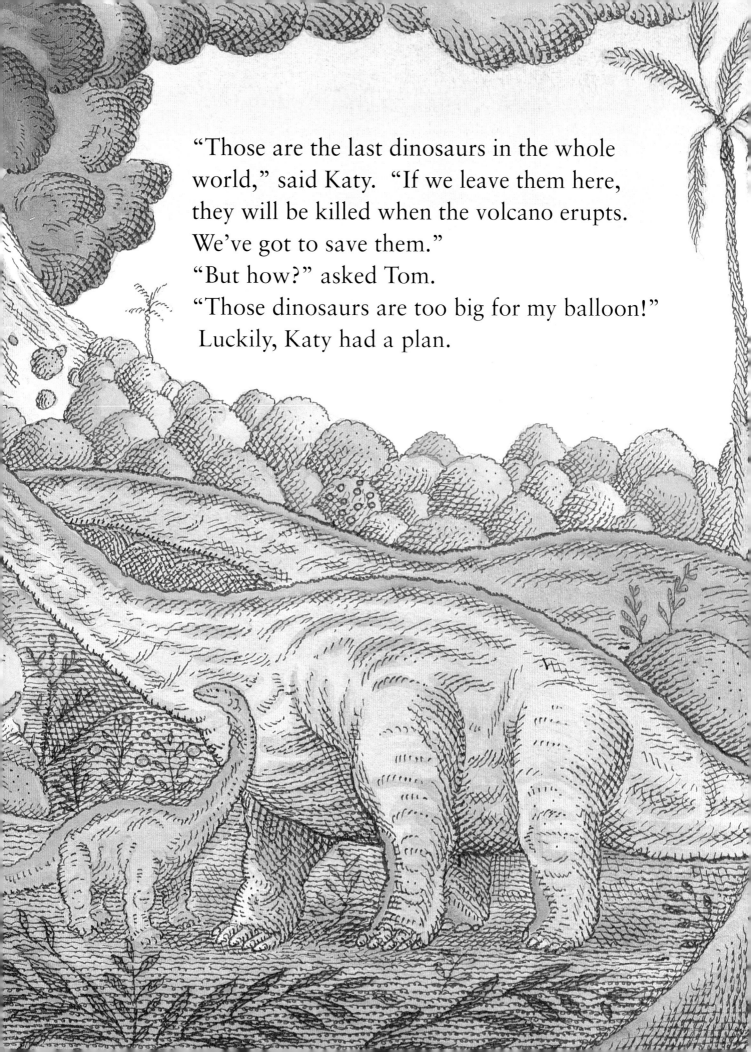

"Those are the last dinosaurs in the whole
world," said Katy. "If we leave them here,
they will be killed when the volcano erupts.
We've got to save them."
"But how?" asked Tom.
"Those dinosaurs are too big for my balloon!"
Luckily, Katy had a plan.

First they collected armfuls of enormous flowers.

Katy knew that the dinosaurs loved to eat the flowers.

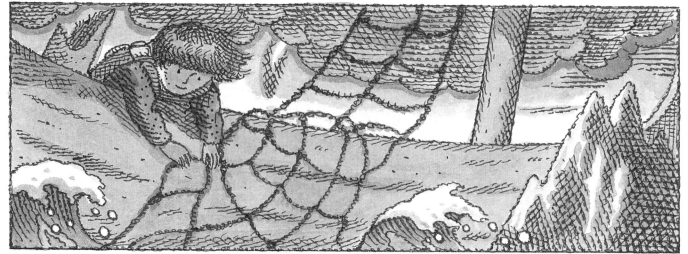

Then they made huge nets from the rigging on Katy's wrecked ship.

Tom hung them from the basket of his balloon.

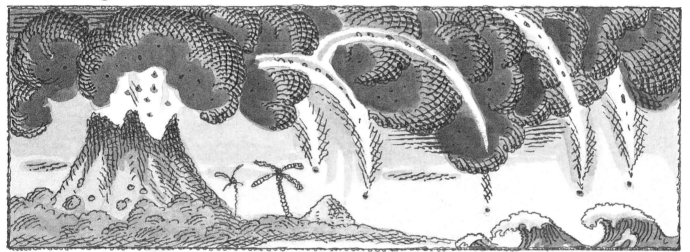

All the time the explosions from the volcano got louder and louder.

They laid a trail of flowers for the dinosaurs to follow.

At the water's edge, Katy clambered up into the balloon's basket and threw handfuls of flowers on to the water.

The dinosaurs followed, swimming.
The plan had worked! The seas turned black around them
and hot rocks hissed down as...

...the volcano erupted! They had got away in the nick of time!

Just as the smallest dinosaur was getting
too tired to swim, they reached a beautiful island.
Then it was time for Tom and Katy to start
the long journey home. They said goodbye
to the dinosaurs and set off in the red balloon.

But the journey home was not easy.
Winds howled round the basket. Rain
lashed over them. The moon vanished.
There was nothing but icy blackness.

Just as Tom thought he would never see his grandfather
again, a bright light pierced the swirling black clouds.
"It's the lighthouse!" he cried. And as they flew closer,
Tom could see his grandfather on the balcony,
watching out for him to come home.

Safe at last, and wrapped in blankets, Tom and Katy drank hot cocoa in front of the fire. Grandfather listened as they told him the wonderful story of the shipwreck, the volcano and rescuing the last dinosaurs.